WILD ROBIN

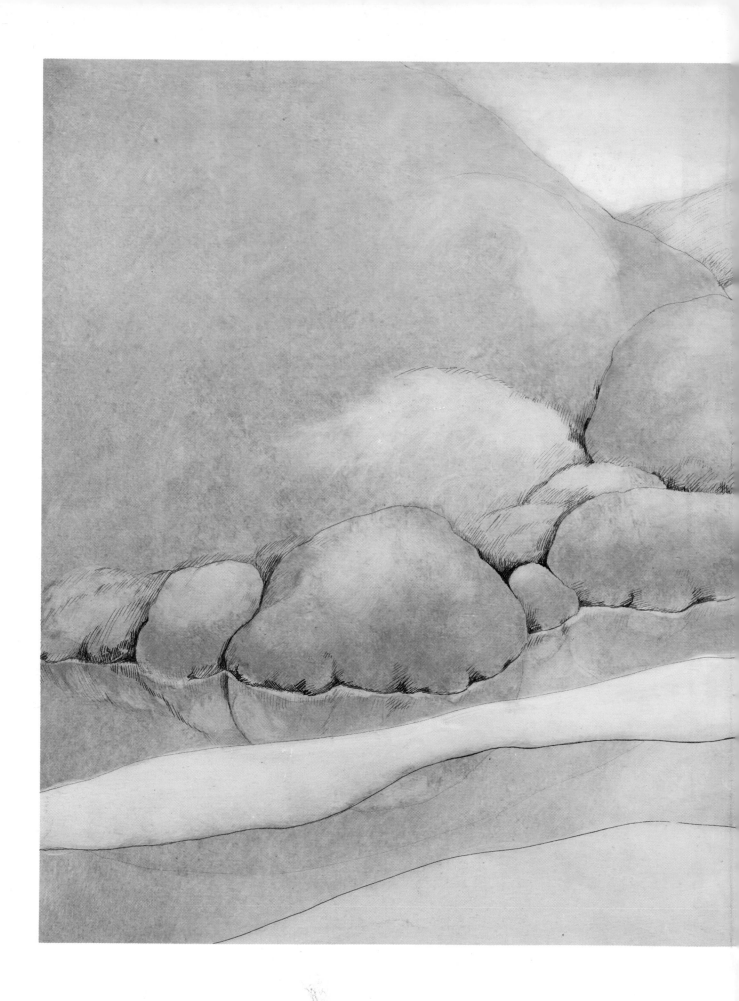

WILD ROBIN

retold and illustrated by SUSAN JEFFERS

E. P. Dutton   New York

Wild Robin is based on a tale in *Little Prudy's
Fairy Book* by Sophie May (Rebecca S. Clarke).

Copyright © 1976 by Susan Jeffers
All rights reserved.
Unicorn is a registered trademark of E. P. Dutton
Library of Congress number 76-21343
ISBN 0-525-44244-8
Published in the United States by E. P. Dutton,
2 Park Avenue, New York, N.Y. 10016,
a subsidiary of NAL Penguin Inc.
Published simultaneously in Canada by
Fitzhenry & Whiteside Limited, Toronto
Editor: Ann Durell
Printed in Hong Kong by South China Printing Co.
First Unicorn Edition 1986   COBE
10 9 8 7 6 5 4 3 2

For my mother, Alice

Robin was a wild boy. As wild as the wind across the hills. He hated everyday things, like carrying water from the well.

He hid when it was time to sweep the barn.

For most of all, he hated tending the cows.

His sister Janet was a kind girl, and she loved
her wayward brother. She would sometimes
eat his porridge for him.

And she would even help clean the barn
and tend the cows.

But one day Robin was more wild than ever.
He spilled his porridge on the floor. He poured
water on his boots. And he refused to clean the
cow barn. Even Janet lost patience with him.
"Well, then, I'll run away," said Robin to himself.

And off he went, over the windy hills.

At last Robin could run no more. And by the edge of St. Mary's loch, he flung himself on the grass and was soon sound asleep. He did not know that the ring of moss in which he lay belonged to the fairies. The water kelpies and other elvish creatures knew, and they laughed with glee.

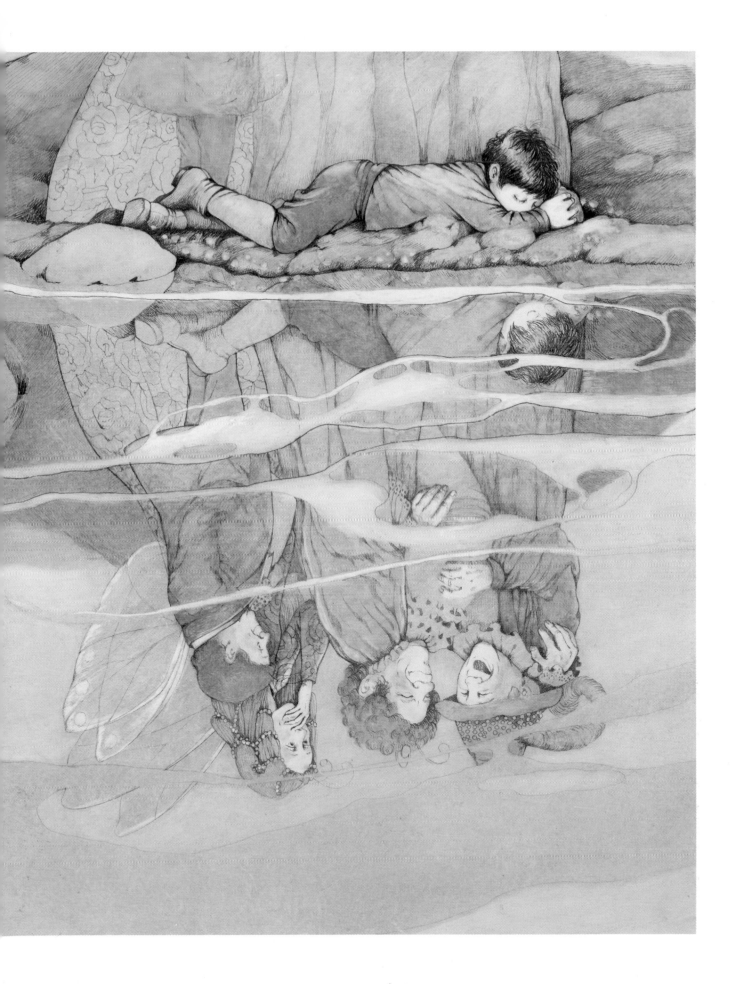

The sun fell, and over the hills came the tinkling of tiny bridle bells. The fairies were riding over the moor.

The Queen stopped in the fairy ring, and laid her fingers on Robin's cheek. "This little man shall be mine," she said. "Elves, set him on a horse and take him to my castle."

When Robin awoke, he found himself looking into the cold gray eyes of the Queen.

"You are now in Fairyland," she told him. "Here there is nothing to do but play and eat to your heart's content."

Everywhere Robin went,
his eyes were dazzled.

He soon found that indeed he could do as he liked. There was no water to be carried, no porridge to be eaten, no sweeping to be done. If the fairies had cows, they needed no tending. He was very pleased with this easy life.

But one day Robin found he was tired of
having nothing to do. And he was lonely.
He missed his mother and his father and,
most of all, he missed Janet.
There was one elf who liked to tease him
with news of the human world.

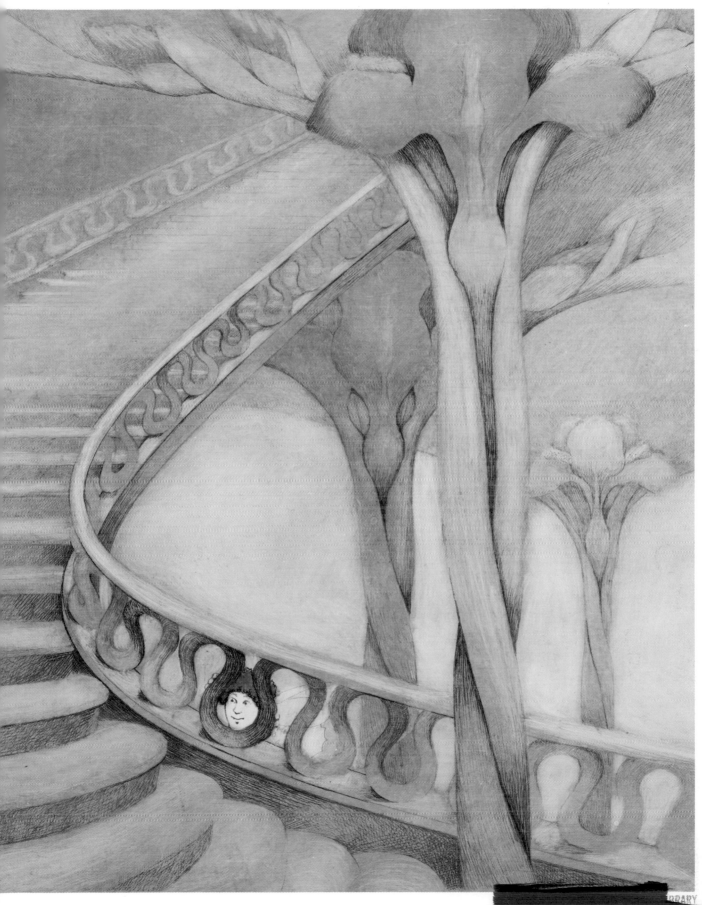

The elf told Robin how his mother
watched by the window while his
father and Janet searched for him
across the hills.

One night when this elf went to spy
on the human world, he did not
see Janet. Finally he found her in
the hayloft. She was sobbing so
bitterly for Robin that even the
elf's little stone heart was touched.

He showed Janet her brother in a dream. And Robin told her how she could free him. She must go to the greenwood the very next night and follow this charm exactly.

> First let pass the milk-white steed,
> And then let pass the brown;
> But you must stop the coal-black steed,
> And pull the rider down.

And then she must hold tight to the rider until she could cast her green coat over him.

The next night, Janet went to the greenwood.
She hid for a long time under a tree, until an
eerie cavalcade wound its way through the forest.
She saw the Queen pass on a milk-white steed,
followed by the elf on a brown one.

Then came a shadowy figure mounted on a
coal-black steed.

In spite of her terror, she leaped at the
rider and pulled him to the ground.
How horrible it was!
Shape after shape writhed in her grasp.
But Janet held on, as she knew she must.

And at last she managed to throw
her green coat over him.

And there was her own dear brother Robin
grinning at her. As she hugged him close,
she heard the angry voice of the Queen.
"Janet, you have taken away the bonniest
lad in all my company."
But Wild Robin was safe. The fairies had
lost their power over him forever.
"I'll never run away again," said Robin.